SPICY
SALTY
BITTER

SWEET

SALTY

UMAMI

SPICY

SOUR

SALTY

SWEET

UMAMI

SWEET

BITTER

SPICY

UMAMI

AF583974

A TASTE
Adventure
WITH
MELISSA LEONG

The family you choose is just as important as the one you are born into. This book is for Margot, Beatrix, Violet and Rob; thank you for inviting me into your family. To my god daughter Dion Mimi and her brother Remi, you guys are superstars! To my mum Hock Bee, thank you for teaching me that food is love. To Maddie and Gracie, remember that happiness is always around the corner when you least expect it.

- Melissa Leong

Made with love by the team at

FIVE MILE

Alex, Rocco, Graham, Jacqui, Claire, Bridget, Sarah, Tillie and Kate

Five Mile,
the publishing division
of Regency Media
www.fivemile.com.au

First published 2022

Text copyright © Melissa Leong, 2022
Art copyright © Eleonora Arosio, 2022
Cover art copyright © Kitiya Palaskas, 2022

All rights reserved. No part of this publication may be reproduced, stored in a retrieval system, or transmitted in any way or by any means, electronic, mechanical, photocopying, recording or otherwise, without the prior written permission of the Publisher.

Printed in China 5 4 3 2 1

A catalogue record for this book is available from the National Library of Australia

Illustrations by Eleonora Arosio

Cover by Kitiya Palaskas

FIVE MILE

We're hungry!
We're starving!
What will we eat?

There are tastes everywhere
but where to begin?
Let's discover them all,
from Tokyo to Berlin

There's sweet, salty, bitter and umami ...
Doesn't that last one sound a little bit funny?
Sour and spicy are just as neat and
together these six tastes are
in foods that we eat!

Just for a treat,
how about we start sweet?

Sweet foods are sticky,
Colourful and fun
Such a warm, friendly taste
On the tip of your tongue

On sunny hot days, gelato is great
From Sicily to Venice, all flavours we rate
Nutty pistachio to lemon, bright like the sun
If we lived in Italy, it'd be so much fun!
The heat can warm gelato's icy charm
Be quick, or it'll melt and run down your arm!

In France there are crêpes – they're skinny pancakes
Shall we have some with cream, and a strawberry milkshake?
Or bananas go well with salted caramel
We'll eat them in Paris, where we can see La Eiffel!

Hot chocolate is perfect for days when it's cold
Did you know it's from Mexico? (It's actually quite old!)
Their version is perfumed, rich with warm spices
Try it sometime, you'll find it the nicest

If you go to the beach and a wave catches you
That taste is salt, like an ocean of blue
Mouth-watering saltiness spreads on your tongue
It's what makes all sorts of food taste really yum

SALTY

Hot chips by the beach are a real Aussie thing
Those little white specks make that crunchy gold sing
You crunch and you munch down to the last bite
Those crispies at the bottom might just cause a fight!

Dry desert country is where saltbush grows
Native to Australia, it makes any roast glow
The salty leaves make such a great seasoning
We're so lucky our land offers such tasty things

Salty snacks are special, there are quite a lot
Like in Germany, their pretzels are served soft and hot
Chewy outside and like clouds within,
but it's their shiny salt sprinkle that makes them a win

You pull a funny face
when sour's what you taste
It's sharp and it's tart,
but it can be quite ace
Its electric vibe
makes you salivate
It adds freshness and balance:
food jumps off the plate

There's a tasty soup in Thailand,
it's called tom yum
It's hot and it's sour –
please can we have some?
It's lime juice and tamarind
that make our cheeks pucker
One taste of this soup
and you'll be a sucker

Roses are red, and rhubarb is too
Those red stalks are sour, without sugar, it's true
But in a British crumble with sugary sweet things
Rhubarb's sharpness is lovely, together it sings

Korean Kimchi is so good for your tummy
A fizzy cabbage wonder, with rice it's so yummy
It's mixed and it's massaged and left alone for weeks
To foam and to bubble, before it's time to eat!

When hot foods are hot, they make your eyes water
It burns on your tongue ... well, it feels like that, sorta!
It might taste like fire, but it's really just spice
Go easy, be brave and it can be so nice
SPICY

On all sorts of foods, hot sauce is a winner
A few dabs of fire make one delicious dinner
On Taiwanese fried chicken or on Turkish shawarma
A little hot sauce makes snacks a LOT warmer
Made from spices, sometimes vinegar, and of course chilli
First, try a dash — soon you'll say "Gimme, gimme, gimme!"

All over the world is where curries can come from
For the hottest, from India is where you'll find one
Vindaloo is a real hot-pot treat
You'll shimmy and wiggle, from your head to your feet

We all love noodles to chew and to slurp
Dan Dan is spicylicious — try not to burp!
They're Chinese noodles tossed in sesame, spices and mince
Its glowing oil tingles, but it won't make you wince

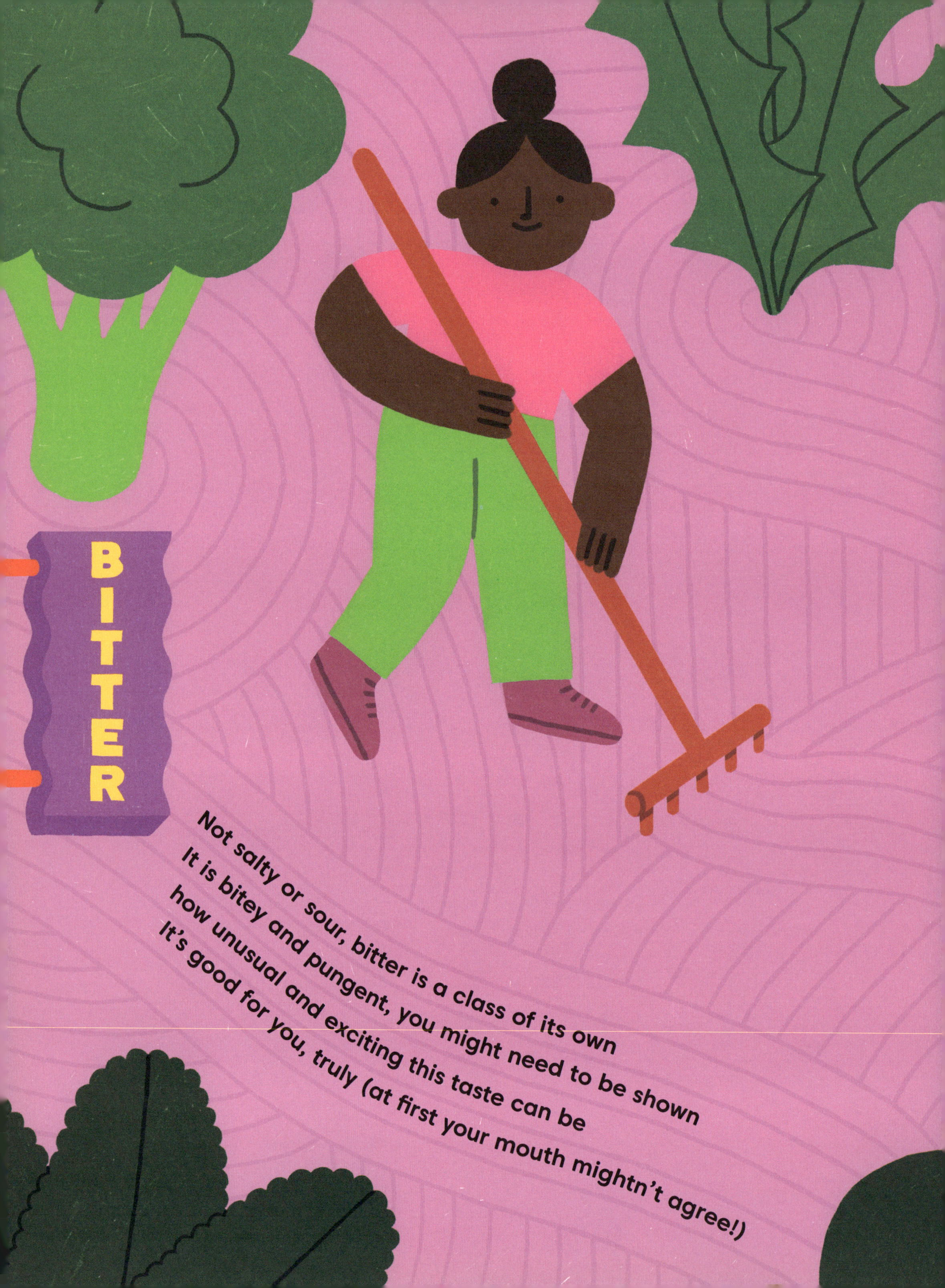
BITTER
Not salty or sour, bitter is a class of its own
It is bitey and pungent, you might need to be shown
how unusual and exciting this taste can be
It's good for you, truly (at first your mouth mightn't agree!)

Matcha is green, it's full of good stuff
That twang at the end is bitter showing off
Dark green veggies are bitter until cooked
They're good for you though,
so please don't overlook

UMAMI
Umami means savoury, with deep and rich flavour
Add it to a dish — it could be its saviour!
Miso soup is salty, deep and rich like meat
But it's actually made from soya beans — isn't that neat?

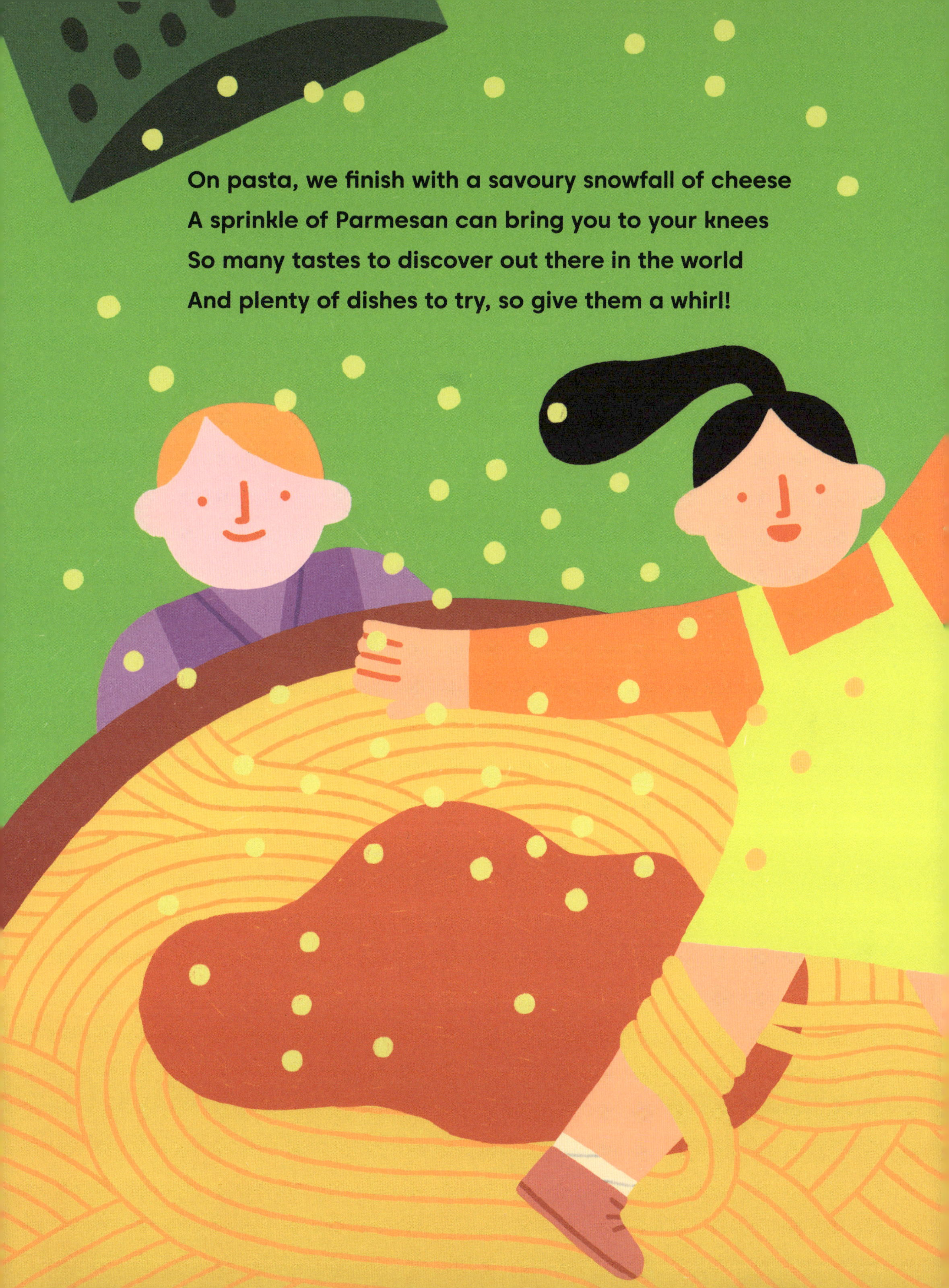

On pasta, we finish with a savoury snowfall of cheese
A sprinkle of Parmesan can bring you to your knees
So many tastes to discover out there in the world
And plenty of dishes to try, so give them a whirl!

We've travelled the world,
through the flavour in food
Some delicious discoveries
you've uncovered, dude!

Now you know what you're tasting,
get out there and eat
Who knows? You may find
your new favourite treat

For the best thing about
taste adventures, of all sorts,
is that they can start anywhere
... like here, in this food court

GO ON YOUR OWN TASTE Adventure

Find out more about the 6 tastes here. Have you tried them all?

SOUR

TRY SOUR ...

Some succulently sour foods include kimchi, tamarind, rhubarb and pickles ...

An easy way to add a sour taste is by squeezing some lime or lemon juice into your food.

When life gives you lemons, you can make lemonade! But you can also use the juice from a lemon or lime to cut through rich or spicy foods. Lemon juice is often used in Mediterranean and European cooking, while lime juice is commonly used in Mexican, Latin-American and southeast Asian cooking.

Matcha is a finely powdered green tea from Japan, where it is used in traditional tea ceremonies. With its naturally bitter taste, it makes a delicious drink as well as flavouring for foods like noodles, rice cakes, and ice cream.

TRY BITTER ...

Some bitingly bitter foods include dark green vegetables, coffee and tea ...

An easy way to add a bitter taste is by trying matcha in a drink or dessert.

TRY UMAMI ...

Some mouth-wateringly umami foods include mushrooms, soy sauce, tomatoes and seaweed ...

An easy way to add an umami taste to your food is by sprinkling some cheese into your dish.

Being a very popular and all-round ingredient, cheese is the perfect way to introduce meaty, savoury deliciousness to a variety of dishes. Did you know that there are nearly 2000 different types of cheese in the world? That's a lot of umami!

SWEET

TRY SWEET ...

Some scrumptiously sweet foods include gelato, crepes, chocolate and caramel ...

An easy way to try a sweet taste is by including fruit, like a banana, to your dish.

When you think of fruit, you probably think of them as simply "good-for-you" foods. But did you know that, when making desserts, fruit can be used instead of sugar? Most fruits we eat have a lot of natural sugar and are a healthier way to enjoy sweetness!

TRY SALTY ...

Some scrummy salty foods include chips, saltbush and pretzels ...

An easy way to add a salty taste to your food, that is also a bit different, is to try seasoning with saltbush.

Saltbush leaves can be eaten on their own or ground up and dried to give foods a salty, herbal flavour. As a traditional bush food ingredient, Indigenous Australians have been known to use the leaves and berries from this native shrub for centuries.

Eaten raw or cooked, chilli is used all over the world to add some heat and zing to a plate! This bright, crunchy and colourful fruit is also often made into sauces, like hot sauce or chilli sauce, so you can enjoy as much or as little spice in your food as you want!

TRY SPICY ...

Some savoury spicy foods include pepper, salsa and curry ...

An easy way to add a spicy taste to your food is by adding a little chilli into the mix. Careful, it can be hot!

MEET THE CREATORS

MELISSA LEONG

Melissa is a Singaporean-Australian food and travel writer, cookbook editor and TV presenter. Her love for food has seen her embark on many of her own taste adventures: from searching through Ho Chi Minh's backstreets for the perfect midnight banh mi, to living on a Tasmanian sheep farm! As a judge on MasterChef Australia, Melissa continues to celebrate tasty food, the way it's made and how it brings people together.

ACKNOWLEDGEMENTS

I cannot begin to express the level of gratitude I feel for the people in my life. When it's time to celebrate, you are there. When it's time to circle the wagons, you are there. Old friends and new, thank you for your kindness and generosity.

In no particular order:

Rob, Violet, Beatrix and Margot Mason, Dion Mimi, Remi, Jojo Gamvros and Matt McConnell, Pascale Gomes McNabb, Leah, Maddie and Gracie Sidhu, Lizzi Dayney-Morrissey, Nicole, Miriam, Noa and Graysen Gilliver Von Keyserlingk-Eberius, Joe Jones, Cat Webb, Rachael Calvert, Hannah Green, Jason Jones, Brem Perera, Jason Grech, Sarah and Dan Swan, Georgia Hackett, Kirsten, Daisy and Evie Douglas, Kate Pearce, Tamara Kennedy, Jordana Goot, Carolyn, Loren and Benjamin Schiller, Nat Paull, Meggy Smith, Daisy Turnbull, Caroline McCredie, Valentina Jurkiw, Yeesum Lo, Nikki To, Freda Rossidis, Shella Ruby Martin, David Forster, Simon Child, Andrew Hamilton, Michele Harris, Collette Dinnigan, Alenka Henry, Narelda Jacobs, Lucy Cardoza, Gary Bigeni, Sharon and Carol Salloum, Chris Crawford, Melanie Chester, Rian Difundorum, David Thompson, Andy and Jock, Kit Palaskas, Eleonora Arosio and the team at Five Mile for bringing my idea to fruition and most especially to my Mum, thank you for showing me that food is life.

ELEONORA AROSIO

Originally from Italy, Eleonora studied Fine Arts at NABA in Milan. After graduating in 2014, she has since embarked on a career as a freelance illustrator. Her travels have been a source of inspiration for her characters and stories. Over mountains of ravioli in Italy, across noodle seas in Hong Kong and down lamington rivers in Australia, she is now based in Melbourne, where she enjoys creating illustrations full of sugar, spice and everything nice.

KITIYA PALASKAS

Kitiya Palaskas is an Australian craft-based designer, who reimagines traditional handmade techniques in her contemporary art and design work. Kit draws inspiration from everything around her, having picked up various crafting styles and techniques while travelling to different countries. Her insatiable passion and appetite for making crafts that are bold, playful and deliciously colourful have led Kit to work with clients from all over the world.